The Seeker

&

The Guide

To Richard + Louise

The Seeker

&

The Guide

with best wishes

Tony.

3/3/19

TONY KIDD

© Tony Kidd, 2019

Published by Bizz-B Books

A CIP catalogue record for this book is available from the British Library.

ISBN 978-0-9574162-1-5

Book layout and design by Clare Brayshaw

Prepared and printed by:

York Publishing Services Ltd
64 Hallfield Road
Layerthorpe
York YO31 7ZQ

Tel: 01904 431213

Website: www.yps-publishing.co.uk

Acknowledgements

Grateful thanks to Val Banks, John Ford, Val & Len Hawkes and Viv Chamberlin-Kidd and especially to my wife Sue without who's encouragement and support this would not have reached the page.

About the author

After beginning his career as a solicitor in East London Tony Kidd was ordained in 1989. He worked in Parishes both in East & West Yorkshire and during that time had six Lenten Courses published as well as a children's book called Sally's Angel. Now retired, Tony lives with his wife Sue in York, still taking church services, writing and is an honorary chaplain at York Minster. He enjoys country walks, reading and listening to music.

Prologue

I came as a seeker looking for the lost ground.

That place where once I glimpsed a mystery and then lost
sight of it.

That was in the days of innocence before ambition blotted
out truth

and gave me instead a goal and targets

by which to measure the steady tread towards it.

Once I could speak of the journey and see companions along
the way.

Then all too easily we became competitors jostling for
position

and forging alliances rather than friendships.

Once I saw a placid pool and in it the reflection of a
thousand, thousand stars

rejoicing in the beauty of creation

and inviting me to join them with uplifted spirit.

Now all I recognised was my own reflection,

a sense of desolation and a grey uniformity.

It was then that I told myself there must be more.

Where is the place that mystery hides itself waiting to be
found and heard?

Where can I see that which I do not understand but am
content to hear?

Where can silence create the exaltation of the stars
and celebrate with the bird that sings its notes of rejoicing?

Is there such a place?
Or is that dim recalling of another age just an illusion,
a fancy built in another time of which I never was a part but
just imagined?

No! For something deep within says "There is more:
there is something I once recognised."

In response you show me a river
and ask me to turn aside from my busyness
and consider what it teaches:
to look at its welling place where, from the soft soil,
it forces its way into the world and begins its journey.

From the very start it chuckles, laughing its way along its
course
and finding the easy path wherever it may be taken.
It will not stop until it finds its place.
It is this that I must learn.
It is the Way I must follow.

PART ONE

Chapter I

A Seeker came to the Guide's door and asked where he should begin his journey. "What is your destination?" the Guide asked. "I do not know anything except that I must begin to travel in order to discover another way," the Seeker replied. "Then we shall begin from here" said the Guide. "Look at yourself and tell me what you see."

"I see one who has wandered for many years," said the Seeker. "I have been to all manner of places and have seen wonderful and amazing sights. I have owned houses and valuable things, taken a wife and fathered children. I am very well off and want for nothing. But in all of this I recognise that I have discovered no clear path. I have grown older but have nothing more to say except that I have been to more places and acquired more things.

For many years I dismissed the possibility that there were things to be thought about which did not depend upon what I could buy or afford. Now I'm not so sure. I see others who ought to envy me but they only look at me with sadness. They should look for my approval and friendship for I could benefit them but they seek their fellowship elsewhere. They seem to say to me 'there is another way,' and it is this that I wish to find"

The Guide pointed to the river which ran through the valley in which his home stood. "There are," he said, "some in this village who have never left its boundaries. When they come to the banks of this river you could ask them where this river comes from and where does it go, and they would tell you that it is a mystery. If I told them that the river begins in the hills fifty miles from here they would be no wiser, and if I said that it flows into the sea, it would mean nothing to them. So it is with the Way you seek: it is a mystery."

"The Way begins in the mists of time and comes to us where we are. It enables us to travel to where we need to be and we will not see its end in this world. To begin our journey we need to look at what we believe."

The Guide continued to speak as he led the Seeker to the river's bank. The water was broad and ran swiftly. It came from beyond a bend to the left in the far distance and was marked in its course by grey rocks. These thrust out of its depth and caused foam flecked wavelets to acknowledge their place in the order of things. The banks of the river were strewn with the debris of that higher level of water which came when rains fell on the hills beyond the bend. As trees spread their branches to shelter the river's progress they also half concealed deep pools. These lay still and almost unmoving even though the strong currents surged only a metre or so away.

"Do you believe this river could support you, hold you up and let you rest in its bosom if you stepped into it? Do you see that pool?" the Guide asked as he pointed to another bend in the river just beneath them. There, just as the main stream sped away lay a large semi-circular area of water. "If I said you could lay in that pool and dream, would you believe me?"

The Seeker pondered, looking slowly back and forth between the pool and the Guide. Eventually he uttered a yes which lacked conviction but contained truth. The Guide seemed almost not to hear. "Yes," he said, "it would do so, and as you stepped into it, your belief would have become faith. Our beliefs become faith as we give them force by our actions. As we do so faith, in turn, transforms us, shapes us and takes us into itself. You would step into the pool as an upright man and, as you gave effect to your beliefs, faith would transform you into a horizontal one who floated and dreamt and was sustained and became faithful. The river would hold you and would become one with you in its midst."

Guide and Seeker sat together in silence beside the river following its course as it disappeared round further tree-lined bends into a hazy distance. "You do not need to prove your faith in this river," remarked the Guide, "but you do need to learn its lessons. Your answer was spoken from your head: you reasoned you could believe and were prepared to do so. But your heart was not much in evidence."

"Faith grows only when reason, the mind and its beliefs and thoughts, are brought into the heart. When that happens its as if we have planted our beliefs in the richest soil. They spring to life, grow and are given force and effect, as they flower and bear fruit through the gift of life."

"So many ideas never see the light of day. We think a thought and then discard it, so it never stirs into life of any sort. Another strikes a chord with us and for a few moments we think that it may answer a question but our enthusiasm wanes and the thought dies with it. Sometimes we have a really good idea but then our busyness and other ideas crowd it out. We never give it room to grow into a belief and we soon forget it."

"If you remained seated on this bank you'd never experience the water. Were you to sit at the high water mark occasionally you'd get damp. If you paddled you'd have some sense of the pace of things, but not much. To really test your belief you need to go in, all the way in, only then does faith have a chance to grow."

Later, at the Guide's house when they sat down after breaking bread, the Guide gazed into the fire and sipped his wine. "You have told me how the first part of your journey has ended. Can you tell me now how it was when you set out?"

3

"As a youth," responded the Seeker, "I tried to worship God but I could never find Him for myself. I only discovered a shadow of God given to me by my mother. She had preserved it just as it was when she was a girl and did her best to pass it on to me. My father had abandoned God in favour of material things which he believed would bring him greater pleasure and happiness. He also sought the friendship of men who would, he thought, benefit him in business. He died surrounded by silent idols, all the symbols of his wealth and success. His friends wrote saying they would miss him but few of them came to see him go. After that even the shadow of God in my mother disappeared."

"Later on I could not come to terms with those for whom leading people to God was little more than a job. If being Holy were indeed a mere task carried out for payment, then it seemed to me an odd way of going about it. What is more, I could not distinguish between those who said they had discovered God and those who had not, other than that some gathered in one place and some in another or not at all."

"I gave up the search for God and got on with making myself as comfortable as possible. I threw myself into the pursuit of wealth and pleasure and determined that what suited me would come first and be my yardstick."

"In the absence of God you became god for yourself," the Guide mused over his rhetorical question and the fire fizzed and spat as it received a new log. "Do you see this fire?" he asked. "It considers nothing but itself. Whatever is presented to it, it consumes or spits out to die on the hearth. It is determined to make everything like itself, nothing is ever allowed to retain its own character and identity within the flames. Even the things it cannot swallow up, this iron for instance, it heats and makes glow like its own colour."

"It is so easy for each one of us to be individualistic and to disguise our isolation by our clubs and gatherings. We turn against anyone who refuses to conform to our pattern. But, as your father discovered, when the only motivation is our own gain there is no spirit present and then we begin to be consumed by our own greed and individualism. Everything that comes our way is gobbled up and converted to our own purposes. We spit out anyone who does not conform. We use people to serve our ends and then we discard them, like ashes from the fire, when they can be of no further use."

For a long time there was silence. Eventually the Guide spoke again. "If we are to begin," he said, "then we must speak of faith. Until now your faith has been in yourself. Your yardstick has been your own success in achieving the comfort you prized. We discover the Way does not lie in that direction when we confront the questions asked by One who comes to meet us as we journey. If a questioner asked, "What do you believe?" How would you answer? That is what you must consider."

The following day dawned with the golden mellow glow that heralds the onset of autumn. The river wound its cheerful way burdened by its heavy load of peat carried down from the hills in the far distance. Guide and Seeker walked steadily along the river bank against the flow of the current.

"I believe," said the Seeker, "that there must be a better way than the one I have been following. I say this because I have followed a path mapped out by the pursuit of my own goals with pleasure and self-interest being the measure of my success. I have wealth but feel that personally I have no substance and my pleasures bring me no lasting happiness. I see others whose lives are a drudgery compared with mine but whose happiness appears far greater. This makes me believe there must be a different way from the one I have chosen and that it is one that brings better results. I also recognise within myself a conflict between my thoughts and feelings."

The Guide's attention was refocused by this last statement. Until then he had seemed intent on studying the path they were following, but now he looked keenly at the Seeker as he asked, "Could you say more about this conflict between your thoughts and your feelings?"

"It's as if my thoughts tie me to the past but my feelings are dragging me forward into the future," the Seeker replied. "I am constantly on the move between feelings of insecurity that demand more and more to satisfy them and thoughts which accept and justify what I have already accumulated and intend to increase."

"Yet you have already said that this response to life takes you nowhere in terms of your understanding of yourself and your circumstances" said the Guide gently, for he sensed that the Seeker was now approaching a difficult area. There was a long silence during which the two men slowly climbed away from the level ground of the wide valley in which the Guide's home stood.

The river's course had taken them in a long sweep towards the hills and, as it had done so, the valley narrowed as it rose almost imperceptibly. More of the underlying rock became exposed in the ancient pathway and the smooth swathes of grassland on which the village stood were now replaced by ones which were altogether more coarse, tufted and sparse. The travellers became aware of a breeze which seemed to have come from nowhere but which now brushed their foreheads with a touch which cooled and refreshed.

"Let us pause for a while and enjoy what we see," the Guide spoke gently but firmly. Just away from the path stood a beech tree whose bronze leaves spread a sturdy canopy through which the rays of the sun sought their way. The Guide motioned the Seeker to sit and both rested their backs against the trunk of the tree. They gazed at the valley path, the village now below them in the distance and the river which was flecked with foam as the water rushed and roared coursing through a much narrower channel among the rocks which sought to contain it.

The Guide produced sandwiches and an apple which he passed to the Seeker and each man ate in silence taking in the panorama before them. After some while the Guide spoke again. "You have told me about your thoughts and feelings and you have spoken of your search for a better way. You seem to have recognised, however dimly it may seem to you at present, that there are many things we believe we want which however, when we look more closely, we do not actually need. Many men receive great sums by way of reward for their labours. They do not need what they receive but nevertheless want it because they believe it increases their status in the eyes of the world. Indeed it may do so for some, but for others it merely shows how far removed such people are from the reality of life for so many others."

"We have self-respect when we recognise and meet our needs but have learned to control our desires. It is also then that we earn the respect of the wise. Your father needed genuine friendship but you learned, through his life and death, that possessions cannot supply this nor can mere companionship bought by business favours and interests."

"Your own life is like the needle on a machine registering an earthquake. It travels to and fro matching your frantic activity as you try to meet the demands of the voices of the past and the imaginings of the future. When the earthquake ceases the needle comes to rest in a steady, straight line. This reflects the silence of the moment in which we live, for it is that which links us to eternity. It is in that silence that we are asked our questions. You have said what you believe. Now examine your answer in the light of another question. What do you need?"

"I need to discover what is true," said the Seeker. "Is it what I think or what I feel?" "Must it be either the one or the other?" asked the Guide. "Are there no other possibilities? Tell me more of your need for the truth in the light of your doubts about the time you have spent acquiring all the things you have."

"I recognise that what I own does not answer my questions and that I need a different view of things," said the Seeker. "The things that surrounded my father when he died looked at him and saw nothing, listened to him but heard nothing."

"Indeed," the Guide observed. "Now listen to the silence of this place, the silence of this tree. Here it stands waiting for sunshine, for rain, for the seasons which come and go. It spreads its branches and reaches upward to the sky; another part of it pushes downward far into the earth and spreads its roots outwards in all directions. Without moving from this place this tree grows, matures, generates itself, sires off-spring and fulfils its purpose. It follows the pulse and pattern of life around itself. It responds to the seasons. It receives some light from above and moisture from below and from them synthesises the energy for life. This tree lives and breathes and has its being. What does it teach you? What is its truth?"

The Seeker had never thought before that a tree could teach him anything. Yet as the Guide had spoken, so the Seeker had begun to look more closely at the trees around them. He now stood up and slowly and carefully examined the beech which had provided them with their lunchtime shelter. Already it had begun to shed its leaves. Thus it had provided a golden-brown glow around its trunk showing the extent of its span by the almost perfect circle into which the carpet of leaves had fallen. Its bark was lined by the years but shone with the vibrancy of life as it curved upward around the trunk and showed here and there the places, now healed over, where branches had once reached out. As he stood back he noted the sweeping curve formed by the tips of the branches which made it possible to imagine a small private and personal rainbow being formed to surround it. There was here, he realised, a grace and elegance of shape and form; there was, too, strength and purpose. The tree had its place and filled it to perfection.

"It teaches me," the Seeker said, "that there must be an interchange within us, a sort of dialogue, if we are to grow as we should and be what is intended. This tree can stand for months and seem inactive but it is in fact waiting with a quiet expectation for the message, which its branches will hear and tell of, that the new season has come. And as that word goes one way, so its roots begin the process of taking and converting and then pushing back the energy for new life and growth." He felt himself strangely exhilarated by the picture he saw in his mind's eye as he spoke. This tall, strong, silent tree full of harmonious energy through spring and summer was now preparing to rest as it responded to the voice of the season calling down its leaves and slowing the flow of life to the steady pulse of winter rest.

The Guide sat silently respecting the Seeker's journey of discovery as his awareness grew. Eventually it was right to return to the path. "You are right," the Guide said leading the way. "This tree teaches us that integration leads to healthy growth. It also shows us that patience is rewarded and that waiting in the present is far better than either living in the past or rushing to meet the future. Nature does not outstay its welcome or anticipate itself. Sometimes autumn is early and spring late but these things have a habit of balancing out."

They packed the remains of their lunch and resumed their journey. After a while the Seeker broke the silence of their steady progress. "So what must I do?" he asked. By this time the path was growing steep and was more rock than grass. The river once wide and lethargic was now much noisier. It seemed to rush with a fierce pace as it forced its way through the narrow channel it had dug in the face of the rock. Here and there large boulders lay strewn showing the force with which the river could flow when the winter rains came.

"What you must do now is to consider this path," said the Guide. "When we set out it was part of a pleasant meadow. Now its covering is coarse and sparse. The surface has been stripped away and we have reached the point where the rock beneath says to us 'so far and no further.' That is how it has to be with you. The Way you seek cannot be travelled with pretence, only with complete commitment. The questions can only be heard by one who is open to being totally honest and prepared to face change without reservation. So far we have talked about faith and you have explored your beliefs, especially the things which brought you here. If we go on you must be ready to become like this path and to face yourself as you really are; is that something which you want to do?"

The Seeker looked back along the path. The village was now little more than a few wisps of smoke from specks of houses; dusk was fast approaching and ahead stood a small cottage which he guessed was their destination. "Can I reflect on what you have said?" he asked. "Of course," was the reply. "Now come and meet a friend who can provide a place apart for your purpose if you decide to go further," the Guide said leading the way to the door. The Seeker knocked and was greeted warmly by one of the most attractive people he had ever met. Quietly, almost it seemed without movement, he found himself seated before a large fire in a room which exuded tranquillity.

Chapter II

Some years later, when the Seeker was asked to describe their host on that evening, he made several attempts to begin but each time he failed. He could not focus with precision on any particular feature which would enable a physical description to be given nor was there anything remarkable in her voice or conversation. Yet, there was about her a quiet radiance, a warmth and peacefulness that soothed and brought comfort merely by her presence. The three ate a meal together which was enjoyable in itself but doubly so because it appeared without fuss or pretence and seemed to bring with it some of the presence of the one who had prepared it.

Sitting before the fire when the meal was over and with a glass of a clear wine tinged with a golden glow, the Seeker found the Guide to his left and their host to the right. She sat with her hands resting in her lap and when she looked at him it was with a gentle and inquiring gaze from eyes which seemed to remind him of many others, yet were like none he had ever known and whose colour he could not describe. "You have asked for time to reflect," she said. "That is good if you are to hear the questions, but have you, I wonder, understood what this means?" The voice which spoke to the Seeker was like the rustling of the autumn leaves on the stone of the pathway yet it cut clean through to the place where his thoughts arose and showed him his lack of comprehension. She saw his answer and continued, "There is One who meets us in the Silence, in a place where there is no time and where darkness is utter and complete. In this place there is nothing upon which to stand and yet we do not fall, it is a void and yet we are not alone, there is no space and yet we float infinitely, there is total silence and yet we hear what is ours to understand. In this place the darkness is so deep as to be like the touch of warm velvet. To enter into this presence is something only possible when we have faced ourselves with complete honesty and committed ourselves to discovering the Way no matter what the cost may seem to be."

She paused and as she did so the Seeker found himself pondering his father's group of businessmen and his lonely commitment to it. "No," she said, "It is not at all like it was with your father. The Seeker looked up, startled, and stared first at the Perceiver and then at the Guide. "It was written on your face and in your heart," she said. "Your father's path, however well intentioned, was unwise. He thought to gain more security but mortgaged his integrity in the process. His insecurity made him gullible and brought him no enlightenment. The Way which is open to you will cost you everything that you have, but only because you will see the need to examine all that you receive and own, and to consider whether you have truly earned and deserved it. You will also consider yourself and your conduct and relationships in order to discover the nature of your own integrity. Remember that the cost of your journey of discovery is not only examined in material terms. No, such adjustments as are needful, arise only because of what we discover within us and it is there that the true cost occurs. When our minds uncover the reality of our heart's desire, when our hearts illuminate the true purpose of our thoughts and we admit who we are, that is when the real price is paid. It is this upon which you must reflect." The Perceiver stood, picking up something from the edge of the hearth as she did so, and gestured to the Seeker to follow her. As he left the room the Guide nodded and smiled.

The passageway which led from the room in which they had been sitting was just as warm and friendly; there were doors on either side and the Perceiver opened one and entered the room beyond. It was arranged as any normal bedroom except that in the centre of the floor at one end was a small pool. The Seeker's mind went back to the bend in the river he had passed earlier, for the pool was so shaped as to recall the Guide's words 'If I said you could lay in the pool and dream, would you believe me?' He also remembered his reply and its lack of conviction.

The Perceiver anticipated his question. "You may bathe in the pool," she said. "It is fed by the river and cleanses itself; it is quite safe." Was there just a trace of humour, the suggestion of the enigmatic smile, in the Perceiver's expression the Seeker wondered, but there was no basis on which he could ask a question. "If you need anything I will be in the sitting room," said the Perceiver, "but this is your place apart. I believe all you need for reflection is here." She stared briefly at the pool then at the Seeker and quietly and without any apparent hurry opened her hand to reveal a small piece of rock. "This comes from the path you have trodden; let it speak to you of what it is to be laid bare in the search you say you want to make." She turned and placed the rock on a small table, smiled at the Seeker and was gone.

The Seeker took stock of his surroundings. His room was spacious but not extravagant. In one corner was a door that led to a toilet and wash basin. The bed looked crisp and welcoming with its white sheets and blankets. Beside the table on which the rock had been placed was a comfortable chair and the Seeker sat down, suddenly acknowledging how tired he was. He further reflected that he was in a strange house with two people he did not know, having completed what seemed like a twenty mile walk. The bed looked very inviting but, as a salve for aching limbs so did the pool beside which were two large white towels.

It was strange that as the Seeker settled in his mind that a dip in the pool before retiring to bed was very sensible, so did a number of fears arise in his heart. Was it wise to get into a pool with apparently no bottom to it, in a room where he was alone, in a house he did not know, when for all he knew the only two other people could have left? He stood up and suddenly saw his own reflection in the pool which was perfectly still like a sheet of glass. "You are here to reflect and to confront yourself as you really are in doing so." The Seeker realised he was speaking to himself. He slowly undressed and lowered himself into the pool. He gasped, for after the warmth of the room, the cool waters of the pool stung. There was just enough room to swim a stroke or two from side to side but the Seeker recalled the Guide's question and kept wondering if the pool would support him and let him dream. His doubts sprang from the rational view that it was sheer folly to go to sleep in such a situation but he felt so certain that the Guide would not have asked an irrational question, so when he had said 'yes' he spoke the truth.

To this day the Seeker does not know if he slept in the pool and dreamt, whether he got out of the pool and dreamt or whether what he recalls actually occurred at all. It really does not matter, but the truth for him of his encounter with the pool does, for it is part of his journey.

Resting on his back in the pool and gazing upwards the Seeker was intrigued by a fresco painted on the ceiling which had previously completely escaped his notice. It was of a young man sitting on a rock in the middle of a desert. The smile on the young man's face was familiar but the Seeker could not imagine why until he recognised a similarity between the man and his host. He could not have said that they were related but they certainly shared the same quizzical smile and puzzling eyes which, even in a picture, seemed to present the Seeker with a challenge.

Almost imperceptibly the Seeker became aware of two things which impinged on his consciousness simultaneously. The first was that he was sinking and the second that he was not drowning. These realisations were reinforced by the fact that he was not afraid, indeed as he descended he looked around him seeing quite clearly the wall of rock which completely encircled him. He examined the rock in his hand, the one his host had given him and which he could not recall picking up, after all why would he have done so, and noted its similarity to that which surrounded him. He also noted that he could see and that this was because a pale light filtered through the water from somewhere far below. The Seeker then became aware of a far brighter light coming from over his shoulder and, kicking with his feet, propelled himself towards it. He found himself in a side passage which suddenly turned at right angles driving the Seeker upwards as it did so and causing him to explode into another pool identical to the one he had left hours, or was it minutes or seconds, before. He climbed out to see two white towels and a pile of clothes beside the pool. He dried himself and dressed while examining his surroundings.

The Seeker seemed to be in a well-lit cave devoid of any indication of ownership, occupancy or location. Indeed the only reason for the existence of the cave seemed to be that it housed the pool which now had resumed its state of total stillness and did nothing more than offer the Seeker his reflection.

The Seeker looked down at the warm brown rock in his hand and considered its surface. He felt no urges to do more than think about the Perceiver's words when she said 'let it speak to you' and so he sat down cross-legged beside the pool with the rock on the floor of the cave before him. The first thing he registered was that he was alone, utterly and completely alone.

He could not remember the last time he had been alone like that. Yes, he had undertaken the journey to the Guide's house on his own but there were folk on the road and round about. He had passed through towns and villages, nodded to people as they passed and had never been, or felt, alone. His situation now was different. He had no idea where he was and could hear no sound and that was a second surprise, for life ordinarily was so full of sounds, some welcome, others not.

The Seeker looked again at his rock; it was alone and made no sound. He saw marks on it, scratches here, imperfections there; he felt its smooth areas worn by time, the action of the river perhaps, who could tell. It reflected him and his situation, solitary, silent and alive. The Seeker almost reeled backward as he heard himself say the word 'alive.' After all, how could a piece of rock be alive?

He decided to put this thought to one side and got to his feet picking up the rock as he did so. There were a number of possible ways of leaving the cave but one seemed, for no special reason he could identify, to be the right one. At a steady pace and conscious of his heart beat, he set off up a gentle gradient along a passageway filled with the same pale light that had illuminated the pool and the cave.

Gradually a sound pressed upon the Seeker's consciousness. It spoke of storms, the swirling leaves of autumn and the waves of winter seas. He had wondered in the warmth of the cave why a cloak was the last item of clothing in the pile and suspected that the answer was about to become apparent. He arrived at the mouth of the passageway quite quickly now; he rounded a bend and there was his first glimpse of the outside world.

The first impression the Seeker had of what lay beyond the cave was of an overwhelming sameness. The rock here was a uniform and oppressive grey and the wind, which roared now, stirred up clouds of grey dust. The opalescent light was dulled by the grey filter through which it passed and a coldness crept upon the visitor like a dull ache which threatened to numb both flesh and sense.

The Seeker could see no sign to guide him. Indeed, as he drew the rock from his pocket, he was almost dazzled by its richness of hue contrasted with the overall greyness of his surroundings. He placed the brown rock on a grey slab as a marker and noted with satisfaction that it glowed like a small beacon securely unmoved by the wind which blew around it.

In the absence of any feeling about whether to go one way or another, the Seeker set off to the right. Almost immediately he was confronted by a pile of rocks and boulders which had not been visible through the grey cloud of dust carried on the wind that now blew directly into his face. It forced him to use his cloak to cover his nose and mouth but already he had grit in his mouth from licking his dried lips. He struggled over the rubble which confronted him seeming to climb as he did so but, after what seemed like an age, he could see no further and was still surrounded by rocks and boulders. If anything, the wind was now more intense; it screamed as it tore at his cloak and at one and the same time it chilled his body and burned his face. He looked ahead of him and saw nothing other than greyness through his smarting eyes. Then he squinted, screwing his eyes to try and make out a shape, a shadow, something, someone standing motionless just at the edge of where the rocky shapes merged into grey emptiness. Just for a second the wind eased as if to draw breath, someone became visible and then was gone as the wind returned even more intense than before.

The Seeker made to go on but in the act of doing so, realised it was impossible. He felt drained by the effort of covering the few yards he had travelled. He knew he must go back. Such was the intensity of the wind now that the greyness was becoming darker with the thickness of the dust that swirled about within it. The return journey was a stumbling shamble with the Seeker moving like a drunken man, buffeted by the wind, stung by dust and grit, now conscious of a growing fear brought on by the intense gloom. The uniform and impenetrable greyness of his surroundings rendered him almost blind. There was nothing to distinguish where the

Seeker had come from or been to, no footprints, no feature, no sign of any kind by which to distinguish the entrance to his cave from any other spot in this featureless wasteland. Just as he felt he was slipping towards hysteria, hearing the wind speak in his mind as it howled about him, the Seeker saw the rock seeming to shine out to him like a beacon. There it sat on its grey slab seeming to be an oasis of calm stillness in that screaming, grey world.

Because he was so weak the Seeker could only crawl towards the rock and on reaching it took it in his hand and went on into the cave. He did not remember the journey back to the pool although he reasoned that he must have made it. Nor did he recall returning through the waterway to the pool in his room although, he surmised, that was how he had returned. In any event he awoke on his bed, in the room to which the Perceiver had shown him and he saw that the rock rested on the table exactly where he had placed it when he had first entered.

When the Seeker went into the passageway, he had the distinct feeling that he was moving into a different world. He remembered the Perceiver's reference to a place apart and realised that was how he already felt it to be. He was confused by his recent experience unable to determine whether it had been dream or reality, fact or imagination and, if fact, how had it been accomplished? The Seeker had been unable to find one shred of evidence to suggest that he had even entered the pool let alone visited another world full of greyness and screaming winds.

When the Seeker entered the room where he had eaten the previous night (at least he assumed it was the night before) the Guide and the Perceiver were sitting at the table and his chair was waiting for him. It was, he felt, as if they had known that he would join them precisely at that moment for everything was ready for breakfast to begin. The Seeker was welcomed with warm smiles and was offered, and soon enjoying, as good a meal as he could remember having at that time of day. The conversation involved inconsequential pleasantries until the Perceiver suddenly addressed him while gazing quizzically with her disconcerting eyes. "Did you enjoy your night's rest?" she asked. Before he could think in any depth about his response, the Seeker replied, "I don't think I rested much." His two companions remained silent and the Seeker felt relief spreading through him as he was able to give an account of the previous night's events.

The Seeker spoke of the pool, of the place where he emerged and of the grey world he had tried to explore. He described the figure he thought he had seen, the violence of the wind and his struggle to find his way back. He also told of the role played by the rock which had been his marker. Throughout his story the Guide and the Perceiver remained silent, listening intently. When he had finished the silence remained for a considerable time and the Seeker found himself contrasting this experience with that of the grey world with its screaming wind. He marvelled at the tranquillity he was enjoying and the warmth of the silence that surrounded him. Eventually the voice of the Perceiver, seeming almost like a whisper, asked, "How do you feel?" The Seeker considered this question. "I am glad that I have been able to talk about what I have experienced," he said, "but I feel perplexed that I don't know whether I actually made a physical journey or not. I remember, for instance, experiencing the pain of that wind about my mouth and yet there is no trace now of the soreness I was feeling then." Again there was silence and the Seeker continued. "I feel even more uncertainty about whether I saw someone or something in that other place and even as I use the word 'saw' I want to say 'felt' instead."

"So you are feeling glad, perplexed and uncertain?" said the Perceiver, seemingly unsurprised. "Yes," the Seeker replied. But if he was feeling comfortable at that moment, the next he most certainly was not. "Where do you think you went on your journey?" the Perceiver asked, and when the Seeker looked at her, she was gazing at him with a penetrating intensity.

Chapter III

The Perceiver's question had remained unanswered. The Guide saw how the Seeker was at a loss to reply and quietly interposed a new subject which diverted the focus of the conversation. "Would you," he enquired, "like to explore some of the higher places today? We can, if you like, go to the source of the river." After some brief conversation it was agreed and the Seeker returned to his room to prepare for the journey. However, the question remained; where had he been? It was then it struck him that the Perceiver had not questioned his view that he had been somewhere so she obviously believed he had made a journey. The more the Seeker mused on this fact the less able he felt to name the place he had encountered.

The morning proved to be one whose blue sky and bright sun sought to deceive, for there was a sharpness to the wind which brought instant colour to the walkers' cheeks. The village below looked for all the world like some model in a schoolroom, the hills above were in turn rich brown and steely grey against the sky. There was an excitement in the Seeker at the sight of the green and deep purple of the heather which covered great swathes of the landscape and, when there was grass along the way, it was springy underfoot. The Seeker took several deep breathes of the fresh, crisp air and as the Guide joined him, they set off.

The two had been provided with neat packages of food and flasks which felt warm to the touch. These had appeared on a table in the hall of the cottage. The Perceiver had not been there in person but the Seeker felt her presence and found himself strangely conscious that she had watched them go although he had not seen her. The climb away from the cottage was steady rather than steep and the Seeker found the journey exhilarating. Slowly it dawned on his consciousness that he was contrasting his surroundings, their openness and freshness, the ease and freedom of his stride and the companionship of the Guide with the isolation, greyness and wearying struggle of that other place. The images rested with him for a moment and then slowly faded but their memory was stored, for the Seeker knew they were important and that there was that question to be answered.

When Guide and Seeker reached a fork in the pathway, the Guide motioned to the Seeker to stop. "I am going on this way for I have business in the next village. Your path is that way!" he said pointing to the gradually rising ground which led to more hills in the distance. "I will be here again towards teatime; go and see what you can discover but do not be afraid to rest awhile for not all discoveries lie in the distance. Sometimes they are at our feet." The Seeker nodded his farewell and set off. He walked for some while; he did not note the precise time but stopped when he became conscious that now the sun was approaching its zenith. What was more, his exertions had produced pangs of hunger. He sat down on a comfortable looking rock at the path's side and emptied his pack using it as a cushion for his back. He ate slowly taking in his surroundings as he did so observing that from this high place he could no longer see the village or indeed any sign of human existence. His world was now one of rugged cliff, purple heather, springy grass and a few scattered and stunted trees and bushes. His companions were an occasional bird hovering in the up-drafts of the air trapped and channelled along cliff faces and a stray sheep or two. Largely his world was silent, apart from the rustling of the wind and the faint and distant sound of a stream struggling along its way to join the river far below.

The Seeker's mind wrestled with the stark contrast between the scene around him in this clear, clean air and the grey screaming bleakness of that other place. Why was it, he asked himself, that here I am alone and not afraid and there I felt so threatened? Even as this question entered his mind the answer began to form; he knew that what was confronting him was himself. The grey place was no more than his own state of mind, arid, uniform and frantic. At one and the same time empty and full of busyness and howling confusion. He had entered another world and there confronted himself. Here on the cold firmness of a rocky outcrop in the fresh hill air he was encountering something quite different. Suddenly he could see the Perceiver. Her eyes were gazing at him intently but also, it seemed to him, looking beyond him. They transported him back to a scene from his past.

Before the Seeker stood a man who had borrowed some money, an insignificant amount, from a float in his control used to finance minor everyday needs. The workman had put in a note saying what he had done and promising to pay the money back on his next pay day. This conduct was contrary to the rules and, despite his exemplary record and the fact that he had a wife and child to support, the Seeker had sacked him instantly. Everyone he had spoken to had praised his firmness and courage; he had set the right example. After all, rules were rules and if a small one were broken today, another bigger demeanour could follow tomorrow. Yet deep, deep down in his heart he had felt a sadness, wondered whether there was another way but the logic of the situation had told him not to waste his time because it was an 'open and shut' case which needed no further consideration. Until today he had not thought of it again, but now he saw the sadness in his wife's eyes as he told her what he had done. He had not noticed it before. He also saw his daughter shrinking away from him and it dawned on him that the workman's daughter had been one of her special friends; why, he wondered, had he not recognised that before?

The scene shifted and he saw himself relaxing on holiday with no expense spared. There were various business friends near him laughing and joking. But there in the background, he had not noticed them at the time, were his wife and children. They were unhappy and out of place, caught up in an expensive charade of which they did not want to be a part of. Why, he wondered, had he not realised that previously?

The Seeker heard the voice of the Perceiver speaking as if from far away. "You have said that you need to see things from a different point of view. You obeyed the rules you had laid down but now you can see perhaps something of the price paid for them. You spent a lot of money to keep up with your so-called friends but now you can see something of the price paid by your family who were always outsiders, never accepted. It remains for you to decide this: are you ready to face yourself? Are you ready to answer the question: Who am I?"

The Seeker stood up. He was shaken by the vividness of his new perception and the clarity with which he had seen and heard the Perceiver's challenge; gentle insistence was how he described it subsequently. He also commented to those who sometimes came to seek his advice that he was aware that what had happened was quite illogical, the Perceiver was after all miles away, but he accepted his experience without question. Her ability to enter his thoughts in this way was paradoxically quite natural to him. He had finished his meal and now moved on, climbing gently higher until rounding an outcrop of grey rock he came to a vigorously flowing stream which emerged from the foot of the rock face. He knew that this was the source of the river which, as it seemed to him now, he had sat beside in another lifetime.

The Seeker became aware that as he rounded the outcrop the fierceness of the breeze had increased sharply. It did not scream nor did it threaten him but it appeared to him that something was being offered. It was as if things could be carried away by this wind which seemed to clear the mind as well as the head.

The Seeker knelt and washed his face and hands in the stream. As he lifted up his dripping head which was quickly dried by the force of the wind, he saw in his mind's eye the tree under which he and the Guide had sat. He noticed its fall of leaves. He also saw the path they had trodden. The pathway which had carried him to this place was bare rock with a covering of tufted grass only at its edges. Suddenly he remembered what the Guide had said about being stripped bare. Only now did he see a connection. The tree loses its leaves to prepare for new growth:

The answer to the question, 'Who am I?' now meant for the Seeker 'I am one who must examine, acknowledge and seek to put right those things which lie in the past but which I now perceive to be wrong.' As the wind blew in that high place it was as if it was beginning to carry away some of the self-deception that had so often kept him from seeing the reality of his actions. Now he was, perhaps for the first time in his life, prepared to be honest with himself.

Chapter IV

When the Seeker left the source of the river he moved steadily downwards and out of the path of the wind. His mind was full of thoughts, ideas and questions. It was just as if someone had entered a room which had been sealed for decades and had lifted the sheets from its pictures and furnishings. As the curtains were drawn and windows opened, so fresh air and light entered to dispel the gloom blowing away the layers of dust that had accumulated over the years. He recognised that he was experiencing feelings he had not sensed for as long as he could remember.

The depth of the sadness and shame the Seeker felt over his treatment of the workman he had dismissed was something new to him and he found it disconcerting and uncomfortable. He knew now that he had exercised his legal rights without compassion and that therefore there had been no proper justice. How could all those whose opinion he had sought, whom he regarded as just and honourable, have given him such poor counsel he wondered. The advice of those men who had encouraged him to be firm was now causing him to feel ashamed. As these feelings grew in him so he walked faster and became angry. So it was that when he came to the place where the paths forked he was striding at a great pace and flushed with rage at himself and those he had thought of as his friends. The Guide was sitting on a rock at the path's edge looking down on the valley far below. As the Seeker drew level with him he rose and fell in with his stride saying nothing.

They walked together for some time in this way until eventually the Seeker's pace began to slacken as his anger subsided and the two assumed a more leisurely progress. The Seeker asked the Guide about his visit and learnt that it had been to a couple he had known for many years whose lives were drawing to a close. The man in particular had borne great physical difficulties with wonderful fortitude and had received spiritual blessing which he had shared with the Guide. The Seeker found it strangely rewarding to be a listener in this way and to discover that the Guide appeared to be valuing this opportunity to speak. What was even more intriguing was the description of the experiences of the man approaching his death. These embraced a number of occasions when he'd encounter light and sounds which he seemed to have accepted as preparing him for his final journey.

The Seeker mused on his own recent experience of sound and colour which amounted to a screaming greyness, and contrasted this with what the Guide had described. He spoke of soft hues and gentle sounds which reminded the Seeker, by way of comparison, of the gold, bronze and gentle rustling of the tree under which they had sat on the journey to the Perceiver's cottage. In a minute or two of silence the Seeker found himself disturbed by the emotion and warmth he heard in the Guides description of his friends. He could not recall having previously listened to someone speaking in this way nor to having felt their feelings as personally. That, he mused, was because he could not recall having listened to someone as carefully and closely before nor had anyone previously trusted him with such feelings. He was left wondering how many times he could have listened but either could not spare the time or did not even realise it would be good for him. And how many times had he heard people speaking but not listened to what was being said especially, he realised to his shame, by those he took for granted, namely his family.

The two men rounded a bend in the path and there, in the gathering dusk, stood the warm and welcoming cottage they had left that morning. The door was open, indicating that the Perceiver had anticipated their arrival and they entered. "Let us freshen up and meet in a little while," the Guide suggested and so the Seeker went to his room.

The pool, his bed, the rock, were all exactly as he had left them that morning and all had an air of familiarity which was comfortable and welcoming. The Seeker realised that he was tired and grubby after his day's exertions and chuckled to himself recalling the Guide's tactful suggestion about 'freshening up.' The pool looked inviting and the Seeker stripped and lowered himself into the water gasping slightly as the stinging coolness received him. He lay back looking as the brown rock in his hands which he could not recall picking up and smiling back involuntarily at the enigmatic young man who looked down at him from the ceilings. His descent into the chamber he had previously visited was calmer than it had been before. Then he had not known what to expect, now his surroundings were more familiar. The pool into which he emerged was exactly as he remembered it and he climbed out, dried and dressed himself. He walked, somewhat apprehensively, towards the mouth of the cave but became increasingly aware that he could hear nothing. When he arrived at the end of the passageway there indeed was the grey world he remembered but no longer was the air thick with swirling dust nor were his senses numbed by the screaming cold which had met him previously.

In a strange way the grey calm was as nerve racking as its violent predecessor. The stillness contained an atmosphere of expectation, a sense that an event was imminent, which was almost tangible. Once again the Seeker placed his rock on a stone at the mouth of the cave and started to climb across the boulders which previously had proved so intractable. Eventually, and without, it seemed, undue effort, he reached the lip of the depression which housed the cave and found himself on a plateau. This lay along the edge of what appeared to be a range of very large hills. These stretched to the right and left of him as far as the eye could see. Likewise the plateau spread out before him broken only by occasional rocky outcrops. The scene could have been described as desolation and yet it did not feel empty. The Seeker felt that he needed to explore but that somehow the time was not yet right. He sensed that there was something to discover in this place but only after other tasks he was to undertake had been completed. He went back to the cave mouth and collected the rock with his mind full of these thoughts noting as he went the deep, clear imprint that his feet had made in the grey dust covering the rock surface. His return to the pool in his bedroom was accomplished almost without his noticing it and once back in his bedroom, as before, he could not say with any conviction where he had been or for how long, if, indeed he had travelled at all.

In the living room, the fire, the table spread with its evening meal and the Guide and Perceiver relaxed and comfortable in their places, again gave every impression that his arrival had been precisely timed for the right moment. The Seeker seated himself and the meal began with easy and inconsequential chatter about the day, the recent happenings in the village the Guide had visited and news from his home. It was not until the Seeker had finished his main course that the Perceiver said to him, "And so today you came upon the source of our great river," and as she said this last word her gaze came up from her plate and met his own filling him with an overwhelming sense that somehow he was 'known'. He realised, even as he spoke the word inside himself, that it was inadequate. It also sounded foolish for there was no evidence for it and was based on a momentary glance, yet that was how it felt. He replied with a description of the climb and enjoyment of it and his pleasure in the surroundings. When he had finished there was a silence and the Seeker became aware that the question which had been addressed to him called for more than an account of his physical journey. "I also discovered something about myself," he said and spoke at some length about the conclusion he had reached especially in the light of his recollections from the past. "And," said the Perceiver, "what have you made of your place apart?" The Seeker knew by now not to be surprised that she seemed already aware that he had visited his grey world again. He told them what had happened to him and of his feelings and Guide and Perceiver listened attentively until he had finished.

By this time all three had moved to the fireside and the flames from the glowing logs and the soft light created a comfortable world of warmth and contentment. Eventually the Perceiver's voice came from the shadows of the firelight and did so this time reminding the Seeker of a waterfall running over pebbles down a hillside. "You have spoken of your need to seek to put things right and that is commendable, for it begins a journey away from yourself towards the feelings of others. You have also spoken of your anger towards those whose advice you took and who you now see as having deceived you by their selfishness. I wonder," said the Perceiver, "if you can grasp all that is happening to you and why?"

After a pause the Perceiver continued. "Your friends, wise as they may have been in the ways of the world, invited you to have faith in them and their experience in such matters. They sought to take their limited view and apply it to a much wider horizon than it could serve. It is as if the scientist were to say 'because I can understand and explain the little I can now see, you must have faith in me when I say I will ultimately be able to understand and explain everything.' Such a one would not be trustworthy because his claim would be foolish and so his petition for your faith is fraudulent. So it is with those to whose advice you paid so much attention; they only considered how an action might affect your business isolated from everything else. But life, as you are beginning to see, is lived out on a much bigger scale than that. Even the rock I put in your hand can speak to you and turn a place where you seem to know nothing into one where you have a point of reference. Many people have been affected by your past actions and your relationship with them has been changed as a result. Others were influenced by your example and followed it and so more lives were affected. The faith you so easily placed in your friends caused their influence to spread like a plague which then infected many dozens of lives." The Perceiver paused and then added in a whisper, "and you did not even realise."

The fire crackled as another log was placed on it and wineglasses were refilled. No one had spoken while the Perceiver sat wrapped in thought. She continued seemingly unaware that there had been an interval. "So much which influences who we are and what we do, we are barely aware of; so to say we understand is to show how little we really know. To admit to being at a loss is to begin the journey towards real understanding. This does not mean that we must pretend we know nothing, merely that we must acknowledge how much escapes us. The mystery is that so much happens without our realising it and we would be touched by so much more if only we gave ourselves time to be open to it. So much of our time is spent being what others expect of us that we do not have enough left over to be ourselves. We copy others, adopt their ideas, arguments and standards. Ultimately, because we have not given time to thinking things through for ourselves, we put our faith in them and then we are lost. The question 'who am I?' cannot then be faced because it frightens us too much; that is because it asks us to stand apart from those who give us our identity and we cannot do it."

This time, as the Perceiver paused, she lifted her head and gazed at the Seeker. "Do you yet know the place you have visited, the grey world of which you have told us?" The

Seeker smiled the smile of one upon whom realisation has dawned. "I believe that the place" he said, "is within me. I am the grey world or perhaps it represents what I am at present." Having said this he suddenly felt a great weariness as though the very making of the statement had itself required an enormous effort.

When the Perceiver spoke again it was as if she were whispering from a very long way away. "The beginning of the journey is indeed from within each one of us," she said. "The Way passes the gate that stands just beyond the doorway of our hearts. There are many who are so committed to those who give them identity that they never even discover that the gate exists. You have opened it and stepped onto the Way. The storm within you has been stilled by the discovery of your need for forgiveness. Now the journey can begin in earnest. For today you have done enough, so go and have a peaceful night."

Chapter V

During his night's rest the Seeker learnt many things. They were confused: there were jumbles of stones and greyness, eyes that sought him out and gazed upon him questioningly, winds and rivers carrying sounds which beat upon him and then caressed him. He awoke with a very keen awareness of a need to return to his home. When he announced this over breakfast, his decision seemed to be greeted with a quiet approval and no great surprise. At the door of her cottage the Perceiver bade him farewell with a smile which spoke of a time yet to come. The Guide and the Seeker strode the path to the village at an easy pace and took no time at all. It was downhill and the village almost seemed to rush to meet them. Again when the Seeker said that he proposed to continue his journey straight away the Guide expressed no surprise and, having provided food and drink, said farewell with no hint of finality. His 'Goodbye' carried the clear message that they would meet again.

The Seeker's welcome home contrasted starkly with his departure from the Perceiver and the Guide. Whereas with them there was warmth and the promise of renewed acquaintance in the future, here there was uncertainty and apprehension. The Seeker knew now that to discover the Way was one thing, to walk it quite another. He also recognised how his time away had changed him. In a few short days his understanding of himself and his world had been transformed. He had discovered within himself a personal world of which he had never before been aware. He had also recognised that it was possible to explore beyond that personal world and to go into another of which it was a part. And then there was the whole question of his standards and values and the way in which they had determined his life. His wealth, business, his priorities, all of these had been questioned within the larger question, 'Who are you?' How could he explain to his family that the man who had left them some days before had returned with his heart set on a very different path from the one he had previously followed.

The Seeker had wrestled with these concerns on his journey home and had recognised that the river, the tree and the rock he had encountered on his journey had spoken to him from the way they were. He had met them and learned from them, not out of any explanation they offered him about themselves, but by being what they were and waiting for him to discover what he could from them. Thus it was that, rather than trying to convince his family that he had something new to say, he let them discover a different approach in him. He found himself talking about the insights he had gained and the places to which he had journeyed. He found it hard to describe the Guide and the Perceiver other than by the up-welling of warmth that he felt towards each of them and which spoke through him when he described his journeys and the cottage with its pool.

Slowly, imperceptibly almost, each relationship within his family grew in a new way. They were hesitant at first but gradually grew in strength as the late days of autumn, full of gold and bronze burned their way across the evening of the year. On the mantle-shelf above his fire the Seeker's stone glowed its warm brown. It spoke to each member of the Seeker's family of the things that do not change and how they could be reached if there were time and an awareness of the need.

In the time of quietness he now observed each day, the Seeker spent some while contemplating the worker he had dismissed.

He reconstructed the events so that he now assisted the man rather than ignoring him, retaining rather than rejecting and seeing happiness in his daughter rather than her sadness. It was strangely unsurprising when one day his daughter told him that her friend had been visiting in the town that day and they had met. Her father had successfully started his own small business which had prospered. It seemed that he now looked upon his dismissal as a blessing in disguise without which things would not now be as good for him as they were.

There were many other incidents in his life which the Seeker dwelt on in those times of quietness. He spent them in what became known as his place apart. This was a small part of a room at the top of his house which overlooked a quiet part of the garden. It was bare apart from a chair and a small cushion on which the Seeker could kneel if, as he put it, he wanted to bring himself down to earth. This place became peopled with all those where there were things which needed to be put right. As the images unfolded it became clearer and clearer to the Seeker that he had never been in control of his business life, rather it had dominated and controlled him. The business clubs to which he belonged were nothing more than places in which to seek solace from a demanding master who took more and more of his time, compassion and integrity and gave back nothing that made him more human. Even the money, which was, he now saw, the sole reward for his devotion to his business, turned into a devouring monster when he contemplated it in the quietness.

These inner revelations slowly altered the Seeker's attitude and conduct. As his focus became more balanced between his work and home, so his family gradually adjusted to a changed member in its midst. All this contemplation was prompted and guided, it seemed to him, by the Perceiver, whose thoughts came to him from a great distance and yet as clearly as if from across the hearth. However, the eyes which once saw through to his heart now focused from within him as did the promptings about people and areas within his life which needed attention. The Seeker no longer saw a face or figure not that, as he recalled it, he ever had done so with any clarity. Only the Perceiver's voice and eyes remained and the one reflected the waters of the river and the other defied description. It was as if the light which had once explored him and revealed the arid greyness of his life now illuminated those barren places and encouraged life.

In his quietness the Seeker had shed tears as his unintentional heartlessness had been revealed to him. He now perceived from within himself that, as the tears fell in the wilderness of his heart, tiny flowers began to grow. Each time in his place apart he visited the many people whose lives he had affected adversely and the opportunities to improve situations he had let slip by him, a sense of relief touched him. Where this feeling came from he could not tell but he perceived that the other person whose presence he had sensed and dimly discerned in the grey desert was somehow a part of the answer. It was in response to the need to understand more of these feelings that he became aware of a growing plan to visit the Guide again.

Chapter VI

On his way back to the village where his journey had begun the Seeker mused on his parting from his family. Whereas before the farewells had been formal and perfunctory, now there was a genuine sadness and a tinge of excitement. It was as if a question were being asked about what he would discover and what he would bring back. He had sent word of his intentions to the Guide and so it was that on a crisp and bright spring morning full of the white flowers that are its herald, he arrived at the familiar door. His welcome was all that he could have wished for and lacked nothing in the warmth he felt able to reciprocate. He renewed his acquaintance with the Guide's family who disappeared to attend to this and that, leaving the fire and wine for the enjoyment of traveller and friend.

Once again the Seeker experienced the silence which made no demands but opened itself to the words it would accommodate. When he was alone in his place apart the quality of the silence was the same. Here, where another was present with him physically, was no different from when he was the only one present in the room. The Seeker recognised with a deepening sense of shock something which until this moment had been hidden from him. He realised that it was only now, when the Guide was with him, that he knew how it felt to be in silence with another. He had not shared his quiet times with any member of his family and so only now did he have a comparison and there was no difference. He knew now that in fact he had not been alone on all those other occasions and it was something he could not comprehend.

While this journey of growing awareness took place within the Seeker, the Guide remained silent and relaxed in his chair by the fireside. He seemed for all the world to be oblivious of the struggle taking place across the hearth from him. His discernment was vindicated however when eventually he spoke. "Tell me my friend," he said, "since we last spoke, what is the most important thing you have discovered?" And before the Seeker had any time to think over his reply he said, "That I have not been alone." The Guide gazed at him with that enquiring look which compelled him to continue. "All those hours that I have sat alone in my room turning out the rubbish of my life, examining the bad memories and gazing on the faces of those I injured by my carelessness, I was in fact never alone. I took the silence and the space around me as emptiness. Now, here with you, I know it was not. Someone else was with me all that time. I also discovered forgiveness. I have come to know that I cannot undo the things I did but by accepting my wrongdoing I feel that I could perhaps improve the outcome. I could also prepare myself to avoid similar mistakes in the future. Now I feel that whoever was with me understood all that was happening and was party to my feeling forgiven. However, I do not understand because no one was physically present!"

If the Guide had heard anything of this he gave no sign. "Have you revisited the grey place of which you spoke before or learnt anything else about your inner self?" he enquired.

"No," said the Seeker, "I have not been to that place again but I recognise where it is and I know it awaits me. However, I have also recognised that the Perceiver has guided me as I have worked with my recollections from the past and I feel her presence as part of what lies within now rather than as something coming from without."

There was another long silence. In it the room seemed at one and the same time to fill the universe and yet only to contain the two of them. Or was there another?

"And this silence in your room, who created it do you think? Was it you entering your place apart or was it already there waiting to meet you?"

It seemed to the Seeker that these words spoken by the Guide were taken up by the silence itself and expanded until they became a great chorus of autumn leaves and cascading water falling into his mind. The words in turn evoked others forming questions. "Whose space? Whose silence? Whose forgiveness? Just as speedily the sounds died away leaving only one question. From somewhere beyond himself the Seeker heard his own voice saying, "I am someone who has experienced forgiveness and discovered a way. Now I want to understand how to continue my journey."

"Then know that the silence of which you speak is part of the way and that the way passes through a wilderness. That wilderness lies within each one of us and yet, like the silence, we who travel the way share what it teaches us. It is the gift of the One who questions us and whose Spirit is our guide. You know something of this Spirit for you have met one who is full of her. The same Spirit who guides the Perceiver will guide each one of us if we allow it."

The Seeker considered these things. A silence awaited him; in other words he did not create silence for himself, it had always been there waiting for him to discover it. The silence had waited patiently until he made himself available to discover and approach it. That silence was part of the journey, part of the way. The way was not just some pathway from one place to another but an approach to life itself which differed from some others because it gave and demanded nothing in return. It allowed itself to be entered rather than making those who sought it, captive. It also offered a path to self-knowledge through the promptings of the same Spirit that guided the Perceiver and a way of experiencing forgiveness for acknowledged wrongs. And all of this was shared; the way began within but all travelled the same path. The Spirit was within him and yet guided all others on the same path. And there were no demands, only the observance of those disciplines which he felt aided his journey. The Seeker reflected on the enormity of this vision. He felt that he was glimpsing another world whose boundaries merged with his own just at the edge of the picture in his mind. It was one in which the greyness of his inner world became the lush green of fruitful summer with silence as its warm and welcoming air.

Chapter VII

"If I am to help you open the gate of your heart and set your foot upon the way then we must look again at your thoughts and feelings. How do you see your mind and your heart now that you have revisited your past?" The Guide and Seeker were treading again the path by the river leading away from the village. The day was bright and clear with the remains of the overnight frost still thick on the ground where it was not yet touched by the sun. "Let your mind see what it thinks about all that you have felt since we first met. Let your heart see what it feels about your thoughts." Faced with this challenge the journey progressed in silence.

As they walked, the Seeker remembered the silence which had accompanied them when he and the Guide had last spoken of such matters; it seemed a lifetime ago. Then thoughts and feelings had confronted him with an enigma which prevented him from discovering the truth. Somehow in that conversation he had managed to slide away from actually confronting the conflict within him. He now recognised that then the time had not been right to go further than he had. But now where should he begin? The Guide had told him to take his thoughts and see how he felt about them. Was that right? Was he primarily a person who thought first and felt later? On the first journey he would have agreed that it was so without hesitation but now he was not so sure. He felt differently about himself because he had become far more conscious of his reactions to situations when previously he would not have given them a second thought.

"I feel cleaner, freer and more relaxed and I think that has helped me to see how the way ahead might be different from the past. In fact I think I see a path that is right for me, one that makes me feel contented even if I am somewhat apprehensive."

"My journey began in earnest when I decided to seek your guidance a second time. I understand what you have said to me about silence. I know that I have changed because I now consider what I feel first and then think how I might go ahead with those feelings. In other words I bring my thoughts to my feelings by letting what I feel inform my mind."

The Guide gave a murmur of satisfaction. "Then," he said, "you must take your first step into the wilderness. If you are right in your assessment of yourself and I believe you are, there you will encounter other questions."

The familiar cottage came into view as they climbed away from the valley. The Seeker became aware that the river was in spate, full of thunderous noise and boiling foam. The cottage garden was white with snowdrops which were passing their best as the yellow of mature springtime began to take their place. A climbing plant which hung about a porch was already covered with fresh green leaves and full flower buds hung ready to challenge the remains of winter.

Before long they were seated together with the Perceiver having been provided with warm welcomes and hot drinks. The late afternoon sunshine illuminated the room in which a fire gathered strength in the hearth.

Pleasantries were exchanged and news imparted and when it was done the Perceiver looked intently at the Seeker and said, "You have come with a need; can you say what it is?" "To travel further," he replied. "By way of the wilderness?" the Perceiver asked. "If that is where the Way lies, yes," was his response. He looked at the Perceiver's eyes and saw there the gaze that he had come to know so well in his place apart and a smile crossed her face as she acknowledged his recognition.

"The Way is a hard one to travel," mused the Perceiver gazing into the fire. "It is a rocky path, narrow and often difficult to discern; it will test and try you." Her gaze settled on him again. She had not spoken in a questioning way and did not seem to expect any response except that which she saw in him for herself. When she spoke again it was clear that a decision had been reached. "Come with me," she said and indicated that the Guide should join them.

The Perceiver led them into the familiar passageway but this time they did not enter the room containing the pool, instead the Perceiver opened a door on the opposite side of the passage. The room beyond was smaller, cosier and less formal. A window looked out on the valley below but more immediately a vista of racing clouds and brilliant blue sky filled the view. A bed to one side, a small table, an upright chair below the window and a comfortable armchair were the furnishings. There was a small sink in a corner behind the door. Another door opened to reveal storage space and shelves and the Perceiver took the Seeker's bag and placed it on one of them. "This is all you need," she said and, nodding to the Guide, she left.

The Guide pointed the Seeker to the armchair and went and stood gazing out of the window. "To begin your journey you must find the gate which opens on to the Way," he said. "The gate lies within your heart but for so many it is difficult to find because they think they already know the way to go and so do not test their thoughts in their hearts. With others they focus on themselves so much that it obscures the gate. It is placed in such a way as to be much more accessible when we are focused on others rather than ourselves. When we discover it we realise why so many overlooked it. They are expecting something ornate and grand but those who travel this path do so in the company of those who recognise the handicraft of a good carpenter. Do not look for ironwork giving access to a grand avenue; the Way is a humble path but it climbs to eternity."

"How do I begin to look for the gate?" the Seeker asked. "By taking your mind into your heart. Think of those you love and for whom you are concerned. Think of what is best for them. Feel the love you have for them and let it expand to enfold your thoughts; then rest but remain alert. When heart and mind are unified they enable the Spirit within you to search for the gate. When all three set foot on the Way together, your soul, which comprises all that you are, will begin its journey. Use this candle as your focus." The Seeker listened intently to this response to his question and watched as the Guide lit a candle on the table. He then felt the Guide's hands upon his head and heard the words, "Travel in peace," and with that he was left alone.

For some while he sat with his mind filled with images of his wife, children and various friends about whom he was concerned. He expressed his love for them all in their different needs and gradually he felt more still and peaceful than had been the case for a very long while. The total silence of his room and the light of the candle brought forth a response from inside him which seemed to permeate his whole body and then radiate out to meet its counterpart in the room around him.

The light of the candle grew brighter so that the space around it seemed to merge into darkness that itself deepened into a blackness of such intensity that it seemed almost tangible. Yet there was nothing in the experience which threatened the Seeker. The darkness became almost like black velvet enfolding and supporting him while the light was so intense that he was forced to close his eyes in order to protect them. It was then that he experienced feelings similar to those he had undergone when descending through the pool. He acknowledged their familiarity but now continued to focus on his thoughts and feelings for family and friends. It was as if he was moving through the darkness and meeting each one in turn emerging from the light. 'It is almost as though this soft and supporting darkness represents my feelings and each person comes to me from the light of my thoughts,' the Seeker said to himself. Indeed, each person who came into his thoughts was enveloped in his feelings and appeared to him to be carried up in a cloak of black velvet which cushioned and caressed them.

As his progress continued the Seeker was attracted to a patch of light in the distance and moved towards it. This area was populated by numerous people busying themselves in all sorts of activity. There was a general movement along a broad road on which some walked and others danced. Yet others were transported in all manner of conveyances some of which were familiar to the Seeker and others not. It was as if the highway was so vast that it was capable of handling as much traffic as there might be and whatever those travelling wanted to do would to be possible. Some bathed in sunshine on one side of the highway while opposite others played on snow covered slopes. All this appeared to the Seeker in a series of pictures as if he were using a huge kaleidoscope. He fancied that in some of these pictures he saw colleagues from his past and that they were beckoning to him to come and join them. Indeed, when he tried to turn away it took considerable effort to do so because there seemed so much to do and enjoy.

However, the Seeker had noticed that his companions to whom he had previously been devoting his thoughts and feelings were no longer alongside him as they had been. So alluring had been the sights that had attracted him that he had failed to notice their absence. As soon as he refocused his thoughts and feelings he saw in the distance a number of faint lights and moved towards them. The effort required to do this was considerable such was the pull of the previous attractions but the Seeker persisted. As the faint lights became stronger so the task of reaching them became easier. Eventually looking back, the Seeker saw that the broad highway was now just a patch of light again and the objects towards which he had been moving proved to be some of his family and friends as he had envisaged them. However, beyond them there now shone another small, bright light towards which they were all moving and before which they eventually halted.

By the time the Seeker and his companions came to rest, their destination had taken shape and there before them stood a small but sturdy wooden gate. Beyond this lay a pathway fringed by a profusion of trees and shrubs. The Seeker was astonished and exhilarated by the richness of the tapestry of colours contained within flowers and leaves of all shapes. There was a mysterious sense of expectancy in the pathway as it disappeared on its wooded way. Occasionally a traveller would approach the gate, open it and step onto the path soon to disappear from view. The Seeker pondered the feeling that he should follow. He looked around at his companions only to discover that they had disappeared and he was completely alone. He realised he didn't question his assumption that this gate marked the beginning of the Way he was seeking and that it was his focusing on others that had led him to it.

When his gaze returned to the wooden gate someone was working on it repairing a joint. The Seeker approached and the workman looked up. The Seeker found himself reminded of the young man whose picture he had seen on the ceiling of his first room in the cottage and he also recognised again the great similarity to the Perceiver's eyes. The young man opened the gate and the Seeker stepped past him. Almost at the same moment the Seeker saw a subtle change in the light around him. He looked back at the young man whose smile seemed to say, 'Your journey will begin here.'

The Seeker felt the scene moving away from him and that the bright light, which caused him to close his eyes, was fading. He opened his eyes to find himself in his room with the remains of the candle spluttering in its holder. Outside night had fallen and the inky blackness was punctuated only by the twinkling of stars and a pale quarter moon. Below, in the far distant valley were dotted a few lights which seemed like pinheads on a black cushion. The Seeker's stomach sounded the approach of supper-time and he responded.

Chapter VIII

The Seeker was not surprised that the Guide and Perceiver appeared just to have sat down so that his arrival seemed to be exactly on time. Their conversation included him quite naturally, indeed he now recognised names both from the Guide's own village and the one beyond the cottage in the next valley. The Seeker had to suppress his excitement since he wished to relate his experiences while they were still fresh in his mind. However, the opportunity never arose.

As the meal drew to a conclusion the Perceiver looked at him with a gentle smile, "You must return to your journey without delay," she said. "We have kept you from it for far too long." Her steady gaze left no room for argument and the Seeker returned to his room puzzled and disappointed. He lit a fresh candle, settled in his chair and went over what he would have said had he been allowed to speak. Almost without realising it his imaginings merged into reality and he was standing on the pathway again. He began to walk, admiring the variety of trees and other plants as he did so. There was, he noted, an abundance of bird life and flowers of many different kinds; some familiar, others new to him. After walking for some while he noticed that the way ahead was now less distinct than it had been at first. Indeed he now found himself hesitating about which way to go. Since a nearby tree offered a broad branch at a convenient height, the Seeker sat down on it and allowed himself to rest.

Why, the Seeker mused, had the clear path suddenly become so indistinct? The euphoria he had felt on finding it was fast evaporating and yet he knew that that was no response. What was more, in a strange way he could now understand why the Perceiver might not have wished to hear from him over supper; after all, finding a path was one thing, travelling it quite another. Thinking about previous journeys, particularly with the Guide, the Seeker looked around him; what was there to learn and what could his surroundings teach him?

The Seeker noted the height of trees which permitted tall shrubs to have a space beneath them. The bushes with their compact branches and dense structures nevertheless allowed for tender plants of various kinds and hues to nestle around them and to have a secure foothold from which to push out. The small birds that found shelter in the bushes and fed from the shrubs flitted about while their bigger cousins flew from treetops high above.

The Seeker began to see the order of things which previously had eluded him. Although going nowhere in the sense of journeying as he was, each plant had its place and purpose. 'What is mine?' the Seeker asked himself. 'Why am I travelling this path? In order to discover a better way,' was his response. 'I want to learn about myself and the way of things about me. I am on the right path, but now I must discover what it has to teach me.' The Seeker had it in mind to retrace his steps and begin again but when he rose from his branch the narrow path seemed so remarkably clear that he was surprised that he had not been able to see it earlier. He put his lapse down to tiredness and renewed his journey with fresh vigour.

Suddenly the pathway widened into a clearing in one part of which there was what appeared to be a garden. No dwelling was immediately visible but the seeker's gaze was so arrested by a profusion of roses growing in a standard fashion, that he ignored the apparent absence of buildings in his desire to look more closely at the flowers. The range of colour was quite stunning and the air was heavy with a blend of different scents each subtly trying to draw his attention. There being no fences it seemed quite natural to explore this natural delight, almost as if a painting had been placed in his way to enjoy. It seemed equally unremarkable when he came upon the young man he had seen repairing the gate, tending a rose by removing some spent flowers. "Aren't they beautiful," the young man said. "They teach us so much." The Seeker had never before considered the educational properties of roses and so the statement was arresting in itself. When delivered in the same gentle but clear manner as the Perceiver's and with the same gaze as a counterpoint, the Seeker was completely taken aback.

The young man seemed to take the Seeker's silence as an indication that he should continue. "The rose takes from soil and sun and gives in return. What it takes is there for all living things. What it gives back is however, unique to each plant and on each plant each flower is itself unique, special to its own place and time."

He took a rose and, without breaking the stem, held it cupped in his hand. "The life of this flower is dedicated to giving. By its shape and colour it gives pleasure to the eyes. As it unfolds it gives scent to please us by perfuming the air about it. It feeds the bees that visit it and will decorate our homes if we wish. We can take it and as we give it to another, let it speak for us whether in our sadness or our joy. This flower speaks of love because it gives throughout its life. You could not give it to another out of hatred, only out of your own love, for this flower can speak no other language. It lives and dies in giving and speaking of love. Love speaks through this rose; it has discovered its purpose and place."

The Seeker bent to take in the gentle perfume that the vibrant red flower offered him. He closed his eyes and was enfolded in the moment. When he straightened and looked round, he was alone.

Chapter IX

When he returned to himself he found the candle had long since burned out. He sat for some time reflecting on how desolate his knowledge had been up to this point and how transient. He also saw with absolute clarity in a blinding moment that all he knew at any one time held good for only a short while before it was overtaken, became outdated and was absorbed by other more enduring truths. As he adjusted to that realization and what it meant for his future understanding of his life, it was as if a light shone into him and for the first time he saw within himself.

Later the Perceiver would speak to him of the eye of the spirit and he would then recognize that this moment was when he had first become aware that such a thing might exist and that indeed the eye had opened within him. For now he was aware of himself as more than a mere accumulation of the knowledge he possessed and the atoms of which he was composed but also realised that he knew nothing of what lay beyond that truth. He pondered how he had allowed his mind to tyrannise him into believing that his knowledge was all-important, indeed, in some ways, all he was.

There was, he recognised now, a need to seek more guidance and to continue the journey he had begun. It was as if this doorway into himself which had now become visible had done so at the moment when he had discovered the gate. He needed help in understanding what lay beyond it so that he could grasp its real significance.

He also needed to know where the pathway he had begun to explore was located. How could it be so real when he came to it having left this room and this chair? He had held a rose, enjoyed its aroma, indeed he could still detect its scent and yet where had he been and why was it so important?

The Seeker went in search of the Guide only to discover the Perceiver sitting alone at her fireside working on a tapestry of a country garden. Her smile welcomed him and he saw sandwiches and cake waiting for him on the table. As she made a pot of tea using the kettle which had been simmering at the hearth the Perceiver asked, "Have you journeyed far, today?" The Seeker responded by telling her about the path, the rose bed and his encounter.

In the silence which followed he thought about his questions and eventually asked, "Where is the place I visit?" It seemed as though time stood still as the Perceiver gazed into the fire and then at the Seeker, before slowly raising a hand whose index finger brushed the left breast pocket of his shirt. "It lies within you," she said. "The desert you saw has come to life now and your inner eye has opened to see it."

When the Perceiver spoke again it seemed to the Seeker that it was from a long way off. Her voice sounded like a whisper. "You have a question," she said, more as a statement than an inquiry and then she waited. "Who spoke to me in the garden?" the Seeker asked.

"To answer that question you need to understand so much more," the Perceiver said. "We have all been taught to respect each individual and each one of us is expected to make his or her own way. We are told that we each have our own peace, as it were, and that is right. In reality however, we are much more closely linked with each other than we might choose to imagine. The truth is that we all spring from and are composed of the same substance as the universe that surrounds us."

"Eons ago the space in which we now live was a part of that great void, most of which still lies beyond our understanding. It was then that the One, in contemplation, envisaged the world that could exist within the void. And so it was that the light of the Presence of the One, foreseeing the creation of the universe, went forth until the One spoke the Word of creativity. The Word gathered together the substance of creation and the essence of life itself and sent it forth in a great, blazing outburst of joyous celebration."

"In this one moment of creation the seeds of all living things, plant and flower, beast and bird, found their place in the formation of the stars and planets to await their awakening as the Word prescribed. In the fullness of time the Word spoke again and raised up the potential for self-awareness and conscience in humankind. All that you perceive, everything and everyone that you know and see, is formed from what the spoken Word and the Presence energised. Without that substance and light no life would exist. Just as the Word was in the creation so the Word and the Presence are in the One. As the Presence I told you about enables the Word to be present in you and offers you life, the Word within offers you understanding as well and waits for you to go in search of it."

The Seeker's head spun as the picture painted by the Perceiver gradually gained colour and perspective in his mind. For him, who previously had only the vaguest thoughts about these things, the tapestry was vast and he felt so insignificant. He tried to picture the One and the Word. As if she had understood his thoughts the Perceiver spoke again. "It is hard for us to imagine the One. The universe is vast beyond our comprehension and we are wise if we just accept that it is so. There are those who probe its depths to try to give it form for us to grasp but many of us can only stand in awe and wonder and accept. The Word however would, I imagine, be very much like the young man you say you have encountered.

His involvement with our world revealed that the One had an understanding of our need to relate to the source of creation. The Word was a response to our need."

Suddenly the Seeker realised that he felt enormously tired. His mind was full and images had begun to whirl before him in an alarming manner. Slowly, after a while, the room came back into focus and he realised that the Perceiver had left. The Guide had taken her place and now smiled at him and suggested a stroll. The prospect of fresh air appealed and pushed the tiredness into the background.

After walking for some time in silence, the Seeker said, "The way ahead isn't clear to me. I am beginning to see how much more there is to understand both about myself and what I am learning."

The Guide smiled as he replied, "The story of the journey the Word made when he was here with us in our world was recorded by a number of authors and their versions of events are included among other writings which tell us both about ancient times and reactions to the coming of the Word."

"There are those who regard all these texts as inspired by the One, others see that what the Word said and did are more important. These records may help you, not just by what is taught, but also by the example which the Word left for us. He showed us how to go about things, how, if you like, to find him in life today."

"And how is that?" asked the Seeker. They had stopped walking and sat now on a grassy outcrop surveying the distant valley. Tiny spring flowers dotted the rock where it was exposed but grass had not yet claimed the space. The sun provided pleasant warmth.

"Partly by his guidance on how we should live day to day and how we should treat each other better than we do. You have been looking at a different way of going about things in your own life and already you know that it feels good to have done so. But then there is silence and using it to approach the One. It may sound strange, even paradoxical, to say so but the Word shows us how we should use silence in order to communicate beyond the here and now."

To the Seeker these words announced something incredible. His life had been altogether earthbound and rational until his exploration with the Guide began. Admittedly since then some of his experiences, especially at the Perceiver's cottage, had been strange but explicable as dreams and imaginings. Compared with them however, what the Guide now suggested went much, much further. He was saying that the Seeker could communicate with the One who created the universe. Suddenly the sheer beauty of the valley struck him and his gaze was then attracted by a small white flower nestling in the crack of one of the rocks nearby. "All this," he found himself saying, "all this." As if he could see into his mind the Guide replied, "Yes, all this and you and me also. Don't forget that we too were envisaged and brought into being."

"How do I start?" the Seeker asked.

"By letting the Perceiver explain one or two of the thoughts and ideas the Word brought to us and listening to reflections on them," the Guide said. "This is not a work to be rushed into, for it will search you very deeply. It will show you parts of yourself you do not presently know. It will, when you set out on this journey, become darkest right before you see a glimmer of dawn and the night itself may be very long."

The Guide's tone had left no room for doubt as to his seriousness. The Seeker knew the option was his. He did not have to journey at all or, indeed, to begin it now. The Guide's way of explaining what could lie ahead made it clear that to stop and consider would seem perfectly sensible. Once again the rose came into the Seeker's mind, the flower which knew its place and purpose. The One looked at the rose and the rose nodded back knowing that it was as it should be. "I would like to begin to learn," the Seeker announced and the Guide smiled in response. Together they began the journey back, now warmed by an evening sun.

PART TWO – MANY YEARS LATER

Chapter X

I inherited the house where I was brought up when my father, who was in his late 90s, died. He had inherited the property when his father passed away also in his 90s and he had in turn inherited it in similar circumstances. As a result what I found when I explored the attic room of the house was an extraordinary accumulation of the old and even older. Clearly there had been no attempt to sort out what had been stored for many years. Although I found it a daunting task I took this upon myself and gradually I made progress.

It was in the late summer of the year that I came across what I can best describe as a seafarer's chest. It was a sturdy wooden affair strengthened with iron straps and secured with a formidable padlock. I do not know where I had learnt about the hiding place of the key to such a lock but with some considerable effort, I managed to lift and then support the chest thereby enabling me to feel along the inside of the ageing pieces of timber which protected its base. It was indeed there that I found what I was looking for secured by two small leather straps.

I must confess that it was with growing excitement that I tried the key in the lock. After some resistance it yielded enabling me to lift the lid and begin to explore the contents. I carefully placed bundles of correspondence, accounts and what were clearly various once valued artefacts, on a table which I had preserved for just such a purpose. Right at the bottom of this collection I came across a bundle of papers separately secured by string and so forming a parcel. When I opened this up I found myself reading the beginning of a story which, dear reader, is what you will have read already if you have got this far.

I readily admit that, having started to read, I found myself sitting in an old armchair in that attic and continuing to do so until the light failed. Then I went downstairs, made myself some supper and went on reading until I had finished. I spent a restless night full of dreams which I could not recall in the morning. When I awoke it was to a mind full of questions. A breakfast, including some strong coffee, began the process of enabling me to contemplate some answers.

I formed the view that the Seeker referred to in the text must have been my great-grandfather and therefore the document was nearly 200 years old if not more. I came to this conclusion based on the style of writing, the spelling of some of the words and the texture and quality of the paper on which the story was written. What I found most disturbing however was the similarity between the motivation for the Seeker's journey and my own experiences. It dawned on me that my ancestor was holding a mirror before me and I did not like what I saw.

The discovery I have described was made some three years ago. What I am about to present to you is the journey I have made as the result of what I learnt then and subsequently experienced for myself.

Chapter XI

For as long as I could remember I had been inordinately proud of my achievements as a self-made man. It has to be said that my father provided me with a good education, but we were not a wealthy family and I could not wait to leave school and begin to make money. I found it easy to do so. I had an instinct for what to buy, when to do so and when to sell what I had bought. Soon my business was a force to be reckoned with, at first in our town, then in our region and then in due course the whole country and beyond.

Before long I was welcomed in all the best business societies, clubs and chapters and as a result, I became someone everybody wanted to know. I got married and my wife and I had two children and it would be fair to say that everything in our garden appeared to be rosy. However, as I reflected on that ageing bundle of manuscript sheets on my lap, I realised I really did not know my children and I had all but forgotten who my wife was other than an attractive and reliable companion on social occasions.

It is difficult to convey just how shocked I was when I recognised in my great-grandfather's portrait a very accurate representation of myself. It was an equal surprise to find myself vowing to change. That was something very easy to say but it brought with it the huge question of how to go about it.

What happened next caught me completely unawares. Looking back I could say that the house spoke to me. It would be more accurate perhaps to say that something prompted me to look at this ancient dwelling with fresh eyes. Clearly it was in need of a great deal of attention since my father had not had the wherewithal to carry out much-needed repair work and upgrading. Nevertheless the building, which was sound in its basic structure, still sat comfortably within its ample garden. As if it were the most natural thing in the world, I found myself deciding that this would be our new home in which I would make a fresh start in life.

When I came to leave the old house in order to go home I took the ageing manuscript with me. On my journey my new-found enthusiasm and my newly made plans began to wane. As they did so, so the obstacles that appeared as objections to what I had proposed to myself, multiplied. Not least I wondered how my wife and children would feel about moving to a new home on what appeared to be the strength of a whim on my part.

It was quite late when I arrived home and the children were in bed. My wife eyed me curiously and asked how the trip had been. I replied by saying to her, "I have something I have found that I would like you to read because I don't think I have read anything so important for more years than I care to remember." It is to her eternal credit that my wife took the manuscript from my hands, sat down opposite me and began to read while I was eating the meal she had prepared for me.

Clearly my great-grandfather's story had as much impact on my wife as it had had on me for it was a considerable time later she laid down the papers on the table and looked at me expectantly. "I think I have got to change considerably," I said. "Reading what you have now read has told me that I have got things very wrong, especially with those closest to me, for a very long time." I paused and when I continued I said, "First and most importantly I have to say sorry to you and then I have got to put things right with the children. I know that words will not be good enough by themselves and that I have to change."

My wife's response, when I look back on it, was indeed remarkable. "You had a very long day," she said. "I suggest we go to bed now and promise each other that we will spend time together tomorrow looking at what you have in mind." I wonder if she realised how little that was but then perhaps it was a sign of her wisdom that she said no more.

That night was a kaleidoscope of images. There was the old house, memories of childhood, recollections of my father and mother and a feeling that I couldn't quite grasp which spoke of momentous change.

When I awoke I found myself alone and so, putting on my dressing gown, I went downstairs. My wife was sitting at the kitchen table with the manuscript before her but she put down the page she was reading as I came into the room. The children, I discovered, had both left the house in order to take part in school activities and so it was that over breakfast, the conversation which I later recognised as the most important of my life, began to take place.

I told my wife Sarah about the house, the attic, the impact of the manuscript and how extraordinary was the decision that I heard myself making. Then I described how frightening I found the prospect of relinquishing my place in our society and the reins of the company I had founded. Finally I spoke about the guilt I felt over what I regarded as being the neglect both of her and our children and how much I regretted what I now saw as lost years.

Sarah listened to all this in silence. It was however not a silence of anger or disinterest but a quietness in which I felt heard and understood. It was indeed reassuring. When I paused and looked at her, waiting for her reaction, she asked me what my plans were for the old house. The instant response that formed in my mind was to start planning and explaining. I stopped myself from doing so and instead found myself saying, "I would like us to go and visit the old place as a family and to see what we would make of it. Perhaps we could make a day of it tomorrow and take a picnic. Doing it that way would give everybody an opportunity to say what they thought and see whether it could work. Doing it that way might be fun."

Fun: now there was a word I had not used for a very long time. Fun is not a word that crops up very often in the business world and I recognised with a bleak smile that fun was not something which had been part of my existence for far too long.

Sarah's reaction to all this was to smile. It was the sort of smile that could fill a whole room. "Well," she said, "a picnic, a day out and fun. Who could resist? I'm sure the children would love the idea and I would like to look at the old house again in order to see what it could have to offer. Let's take that as our starting point as a family. In the meanwhile why don't you think about how you would tackle what you have said about the business and what it would mean for us looking to the future."

It is strange how deciding to look at things differently can have the effect of changing what we see when we look at something which was previously familiar. There was a room in our house called 'The Study'. To all intents and purposes that room is an extension of my office in our headquarters building. It was fully equipped with all the modern gadgetry of the world in which we live our business lives. Following Sarah's suggestion I now went to sit and think about the future in that room. I must have gone to sit in that room hundreds if not thousands of times over the years, but on that day when I opened the door, the room seemed cold and uninviting. The flashing screens did not convey their usual buzz of excitement and my luxurious chair behind the impressive desk looked almost uncomfortable. It was going to be, I decided, a long, long day.

It is one thing to set the life of a company in motion, but quite another to escape from its clutches once it has grown to the extent that mine had. I say 'mine' for I was still the majority shareholder even though a number of others also had significant holdings. As I sat there thinking about the way ahead I reflected that it was indeed fortunate that my emergency planning had ensured that there were at least three people who could take over from me at short notice if need be. In some ways I had always seen this as being the most important responsibility a managing director had. In my own case it was even more important since I was also the company's chairman.

It was while considering the leadership issue I would leave behind if I went, that I realised the financial matters had to be addressed first. It was then that I took a decision from which there would be no going back. I resolved to contact the one person in the business world whose integrity I totally respected. John worked in the financial sector and had on a number of occasions been instrumental in finding new shareholders and raising funds when expansion required. I telephoned him and told him there was a matter that was highly personal and urgent that I needed to discuss with him. Without any hesitation John said he would be with me within the hour. The process of change had started in earnest.

I then took a much-needed break from my deliberations and found Sarah in the garden. I was carrying a tray bearing a coffee which was her preference and the tea which was my own. We had a table with four chairs around it beneath an old apple tree and it was there that I put down the tray and Sarah came to join me. I took Sarah's hand in mine and told her that John was coming round to visit and that when he had done so there would be no going back. Sarah squeezed my hand, smiled and pointed out to me how well the hydrangea was doing in a nearby bed of flowers. Not for the first time I had to quell my natural reaction of annoyance that she had not responded to my news with enthusiasm, because I suddenly recognised that that is exactly what she had done. That hydrangea had been a gift from me to her and it was doing well! This small sequence of events, when I tell it like this, seem to be so unimportant and yet it was of the utmost significance because I was recognising a new receptivity and awareness on my part and it took some getting used to.

In what appeared to take an age but, in reality was a few seconds, my mind took in the spectrum of pinks, blues and reds of the shrub. I registered the perfection of its shape and proportion and realised that I was being shown the true value of my life's companion and my need for gratitude. It was an altogether uplifting as well as humbling moment.

Chapter XII

When John arrived he and I settled down in the easy chairs on either side of the fireplace in the study. I told him that at this stage I would be grateful if he would not press me on the reasons for the decision that I had reached and he nodded and left it at that. I then explained that I intended to relinquish both my positions in my company and my shareholding, but to do so I needed his help in complete confidence. To this he responded by saying, "You have it."

There is no need to go into detail about the arrangements that were put in place that day. Suffice it to say that a family trust took care of Sarah and our children for the future and I was left with sufficient cash and shares to enable me to manoeuvre a smooth transition out of the company. I consulted John on which of my three lieutenants he felt should replace me. That brought a wry smile but after some discussion a name emerged and I contacted that person after John and I had had a light lunch. Incidentally I had dealt with the question of who would succeed me as chairman of the company when John agreed to accept that position bearing in mind that as the trustee of the bulk of my shareholding and representing my family as a result, he would be very well-placed to do so. The pieces were falling into place.

By late afternoon my successor as managing director of the company had been acquainted with his new role. He had a strong cup of tea to recover from the surprise, not to say shock and had been sworn to secrecy until I had had the opportunity of talking to an emergency Board Meeting. I called that meeting for 9 o'clock on the following Monday morning, this being a Saturday. Having done so I closed the study door and put on the answer-phone as I did so and went to join my family for afternoon tea, an action on my part which produced some very quizzical looks from our children Peter and Elizabeth.

When I reflected on the matter I came to the conclusion that I was extremely fortunate that Peter aged 12 and Elizabeth aged 11 respectively, were as mature and balanced as they were. The more I thought about it the more I realised that I had a great deal to thank Sarah for in the way she had managed and nurtured our family in the face of what amounted to an absent father. Now at the tea table I was confronted by questioning glances from both children and a wife who said, "I believe there is something you want to mention isn't there?"

Once again I faced the fact that there was no going back. "You remember granddad's old place," I began. "Well, I spent some time there yesterday looking round and I began wondering if it wasn't time for a move. I also want to trust you with a piece of information that only two other people know about apart from your mother. I have decided to stand down from my job and to take some time thinking about the next part of my life. I want us to be in this together so I want to know whether you could be with me to help me do that?"

There, I thought to myself, I've said it. I could feel my heart pounding in my chest and I felt a bit light-headed. Thank goodness Sarah came to my aid. "We thought about going over to the house tomorrow," she said. "We can take a picnic and make a day of it. You can have a good look round and see what you make of it. The house will need a lot doing to it but then that's part of the fun." She added these few words lightly and it seemed to break the tension such that the children expressed enthusiasm.

The day dawned bright and sunny and was just the sort of weather for viewing a house. Peter and Elizabeth spent a fair amount of time debating and negotiating over their choices of bedroom while Sarah studied the kitchen and made lots of notes. I, meanwhile, looked at the three reception rooms the smallest of which had, when I lived in the house as a boy, been a library and my father's study. We all met up in the garden which the children obviously enjoyed exploring and about which they had some remarkably good ideas. One of these was that we should try to be as self-sufficient as possible, something which they wanted to help with.

It was while we were all sitting round our small collapsible table eating lunch that the voice of the stranger interrupted us. "Mr Weston?" he enquired. I explained that although I was a Mr Weston, my father, who had owned the property, had recently died and that we were visiting as part of the process of deciding what to do next. Our visitor was a tall man, quite weather-beaten and about the same age as myself if I judged correctly. He obviously spent far more time out of doors than I did and had clearly travelled some distance, to judge by the way he was dressed. Sarah was quick to pick up on this and suggested that the children went off to continue their explorations and then invited the stranger to sit down, offering him a sandwich and a drink as she did so.

"By a strange coincidence my father also died recently," the stranger observed, "and amongst his papers I found a lengthy exchange of correspondence going back over many years between my great-grandfather and the person I take to be your great-grandfather. Obviously they had met and journeyed extensively over the years. I confess to having been intrigued by what I've read and wonder, in the circumstances, whether you can shed any light on my discovery?"

Chapter XIII

There are those moments in life, when one recognises instinctively that one has reached a major fork in the road. I was very conscious of the fact that both the stranger, who had introduced himself as David Finch, and Sarah were studying me intently. After what seemed to me to be an eternity, but in reality was probably only a few seconds, I decided to follow my instinct and said, "I have discovered among my father's papers a manuscript which gives an account from a very personal perspective of the encounters to which I think you are referring. I believe the three of us should discuss this further." When I glanced at Sarah as I was saying this, she nodded and smiled approval which I found very reassuring.

Since our visitor had other calls to make, we exchanged addresses and telephone numbers and agreed that as soon as Sarah had finished typing up the manuscript we should send David a copy and then make arrangements for a further meeting. It seemed that Pond House, as Peter and Elizabeth had named my father's property having discovered a pond amongst the trees at the bottom of the garden, was a convenient central point and so when the time came, the general consensus was that we should meet there to continue our conversation.

The next few days were ones of intense activity. Sarah and I had agreed, with input from the children, various changes to Pond House and on its general renovation. Therefore we had to track down tradesmen to do the work and to get things under way. At the same time our existing property was put on the market with all that that entails. While all this was going on I found myself in demand at the office playing my part in the many meetings and other arrangements generated by my imminent departure.

Somehow in the midst of our frenetic activity Sarah found time to complete my great-grandfather's manuscript with a copy sent off to David Finch as we had promised. In the accompanying letter we invited him to contact us once he had read the document and was ready for further conversation. I found myself reflecting with both apprehension and excitement about all the changes which seemed contemporaneously to be coming to pass. I was also greatly intrigued by the insights I gleaned from my great-grandfather's letters. It was not correspondence that seemed to require a reply but a collection of reflections on the discoveries he had made during his visits to David's great-grandfather Jethro Finch. I confess to being greatly intrigued by these insights into my forebear's journey and the changes that had been wrought in his outlook on life.

My children had themselves not been inactive during this time of change and I suppose it should have come as no surprise when Sarah and I were invited to a 'presentation'. Peter and Elizabeth, with judicious use of a computer, put forward a very cogent and, indeed, intriguing argument for continuing their education at home. This came as a complete revelation to me as someone who had never heard of such a thing. However, from the way it was put forward, it made a lot of sense, so Sarah and I agreed we would think about it.

It was around this time that Sarah came across the title deeds to Pond House at the back of a cupboard in the attic. We were taken aback to discover that we owned three fields beyond the house which were let out to an adjoining farmer. What was even more interesting was that a little while later we learnt that they were now surplus to the needs of the farm and that we therefore had a new feature to include in our plans, namely, extra land.

We had no difficulty in finding tradesmen to work on Pond House and so the refurbishment got under way. When our existing house sold fairly quickly we began packing up in readiness to move. I have to be fair here and say that most of the work fell on Sarah and the children while I attended to all the legal niceties associated with the move and with my departure from the business world. Our agreement to see how home education would work seemed to delight Peter and Elizabeth who had buckled down to packing with enthusiasm as well as planning with Sarah for the deployment of the three fields. From snatches of conversation I gleaned that this would involve something called 'permaculture' and a range of animals who would enjoy being 'free range'. I contented myself with the knowledge that I would learn more when the time was right.

It was in the midst of this state of turmoil and excitement that a letter arrived from David Finch which indicated that he was ready to meet up whenever it suited us. It was at breakfast that we had read the letter and it was Elizabeth who came up with an interesting suggestion. "Since we are practically packed up here and Pond House won't be ready for a week or so why can't we go and stay somewhere near the Finches for a few days break?" It was a good idea, well received by us all and so it was agreed and easily arranged. Thus it came to pass that we left our old house and, in effect, went on holiday planning to arrive at Pond House and unpack when it was ready, a risky but exciting prospect.

I think it sufficient to say that we all enjoyed our visit to this new part of the country. For me however lurking beneath the surface, and probably arising from all the change and busyness of the past few weeks, was my own restlessness and the increasing need I felt to retrace my great-grandfather's steps. Sarah seemed to sense this instinctively and encouraged me to go with David Finch when he suggested a viewing of the Perceiver's cottage which had just come on to the market for sale.

The date and time were agreed. Fortunately not only did the Finches have a family much the same as ours but the four children seemed to get on well together. Furthermore Sarah and Audrey Finch had found enough in common to make conversation very easy and relaxed. Thus David and I set off in good spirits and began our journey up the river valley to which my great-grandfather had referred.

Because David Finch had a good relationship with the estate agent who was handling the sale of the Perceiver's cottage, he had been able to borrow a set of keys so that we could look around it. The property was in fact known as 'Valley View' and when we went in we found that it contained much of the furniture that my great-grandfather had referred to and which appeared to date from the time the cottage was built. So it was that we were able to settle ourselves down and have an early lunch which we had brought with us.

I think I mentioned that Pond House had spoken to me or so it seemed. By comparison Valley View positively shouted. The room in which we were sitting was filled with voices, so much so that the volume was almost overwhelming. "So much has gone on here involving so many people," I observed. I was speaking to myself but David seemed to understand. "So many journeys," he said after which we sat in silence for a while and gradually became used to our surroundings and circumstances.

Suddenly I had an overwhelming urge to go in search of the room which had the pool in it and so I got up telling David that I was going to explore, and I left him to his own thoughts. I went down a passageway which led to a door which I opened and there it was, the pool, a wooden bedstead, a chair and a table just as my great-grandfather had described them. What caught my eye most however was that on the table was the stone which had played such an important part in his travels from this room. Although the temptation to dive into the pool had been powerful, instead I decided to sit down in the chair and pick up the stone feeling its smoothness and admiring its warmth and mellow colour.

Whether it was a reaction to our journey, the impact of the cottage itself or my recollections of my great-grandfather's experiences I cannot say, but suddenly I had an overwhelming sensation that I had in fact immersed myself in the pool. The effect of this was extraordinary because I suddenly felt the guilt that I carried for all the hurt caused by my conduct over the years lifted from me as if it had been washed away. In almost the same instant I saw what seemed like a new part of myself which carried with it a much greater awareness of the importance of the feelings of those around me. I said to myself, 'I must find that path with its wooden gate. I need to journey.'

A moment or so later it seemed the sun's journey brought it to a point where it's rays blazed through the window of the room where I sat and I realised that I must rejoin David. When I saw him again I knew immediately that he too had been changed by our surroundings and the spirit within them. He looked at me and said, "I must find a way of buying this place because we must not let its history and all that it can teach us become lost." I noted the 'I' and 'we' and with the new awareness that had opened within me I understood that I would be involved in this. At the same time I also knew that I needed to speak to Sarah before deciding how that could come about.

I responded to David by saying, "I'm sure you are right and I am also certain that I can be of help. However, I think it would be good if we were to talk to Audrey and Sarah about what we have in mind because they will need to be involved. Let's get back and bring them up to date shall we?" David agreed and so we began the downhill trek with Valley View watching us on our way. I suppose I should not have been surprised that Sarah had news for me when I rejoined her at the cottage where we were staying. Firstly she told me that we had all been invited to have an evening meal with the Finches and secondly that she had been speaking to our solicitor who had imparted some startling news.

I should mention at this point that the solicitor we had used had also been my father's solicitor and that the same firm had represented his father. Apparently my great-grandfather's estate had also been handled by the same firm and a trust had been created when he died. The benefit of this had passed to my grandfather and after him to my father, but for whatever reason, neither of them had made use of its resources. So it was that the funds had been accumulating for over a hundred years and I was now the beneficiary of them.

Sarah and I talked for some time about how to use this unexpected resource and we came to the conclusion that having it available for Valley View and whatever became of the land around Pond House, as the children's plans unfolded, would be a good idea. We had a most enjoyable evening during which we agreed with David and Audrey that we would establish a trust to acquire and look after Valley View. It made sense that Sarah and I would look after the purchase of the property and deal with the issues relating to its fabric, while the Finches would consider and plan for its use as a resource for folk on a spiritual journey. Sarah and I agreed that we would happily play a part in what went on at Valley View and, indeed, I noted how enthusiastic Sarah was about this. I also observed that Sarah and Audrey had already established a very good rapport in support of the 'Valley View idea' if I may call it that.

So it was that when Sarah, I and the children came to say our farewells we did so, it seemed, as old friends not as folk who had only recently become acquainted. It seemed that the past had projected itself into the present in a quite remarkable and practical way. I should add that James and Lucy, Audrey and David's children, had already been so enthused about self-sufficiency and permaculture that home education and a visit to us were already in their advanced stages of planning.

As I reviewed all these plans and events, it suddenly dawned on me that I had already been brought to the gate at the beginning of the narrow path. The most remarkable thing however was the realisation that it was Sarah who was holding that gate open for me and that was the most humbling experience of them all.

Epilogue

Our spiritual journeys can begin in the most unexpected ways and the gateway to our soul can be held open by someone we least expect to do this. Looking back it seems to me that it is all a matter of awareness on our part that the present way of things may not be the only possibility.

If our world is circumscribed by being tied to earplugs and our eyes riveted to screens, then we may not hear when we are called or see the gate being held open for us. Nor, it needs to be said, may we observe what the world about us has to teach us.

May our eyes and ears be open to see and hear where the footsteps of those who care about us are heading.